For Stephanie • N.S.

For my parents • A.N.

Text copyright © 1954 by Norma Simon
Illustrations copyright © 1995 by Alexi Natchev

First Edition 1995

Library of Congress Cataloging-in-Publication Data
Simon, Norma.
Wet world / Norma Simon; illustrated by Alexi Natchev.—1st ed.
Summary: Describes a little girl's activities on a wet, wet, wet day.
ISBN 1-56402-190-4
[1. Rain and rainfall—Fiction.] I. Natchev, Alexi, ill. II. Title.
PZ7.S6053We 1995
[E]—dc20 94-25702

2 4 6 8 10 9 7 5 3 1

Printed in Italy

The pictures in this book were done in watercolor.

Candlewick Press
2067 Massachusetts Avenue
Cambridge, Massachusetts 02140

Norma Simon

WET WORLD

illustrated by Alexi Natchev

CANDLEWICK PRESS
CAMBRIDGE, MASSACHUSETTS

**A wet world waited
when I woke up
this morning**

wet windows

wet trees

wet leaves

wet rooftops

wet street

wet grass

wet world

A warm breakfast
waited when
I went down
the stairs

warm toast

warm cereal

warm cocoa

warm tummy

A stiff raincoat
slipped on my stiff arms

Shiny high boots
over my shiny shoes

Hat

coat

boots

Out to the
wet world

I walked on the wet world

Wet ground pulls my boots

Wet sidewalk splashes my boots

Wet rain sprinkles my hat

Wet rain drips down my coat

Wet cars swish down my road

Windshield wipers wipe the wet

Whish   whish
  whish   whish
      Whish away the wet

Wet puddles cover wet boots
Dry feet in wet boots
Dry arms in wet coat
Dry head in wet hat
Dry me
Wet world

A warm world waited when I went home
warm mother
warm father
warm stove

A wet world waited
outside my window
A warm bed waited
inside my room

A warm kiss kissed me
And now I'm in bed

I wonder what world

will wait in the morning

Good night
wet world